A Fish Called
BAD
EYES

Larry Golicz

ISBN: 978-1-4834-7886-9 (sc)
ISBN: 978-1-4834-7885-2 (e)

Lulu Publishing Services rev. date: 4/13/2018

DEDICATION

This story is dedicated to my five grandchildren, especially Kaitlyn, and to all of the grandchildren of the world. Their imagination, curiosity, and energy bless our future, and provide the greatest heartfelt warmth and satisfaction to us, their grandparents.

I encourage their keen sense of watching and wondering about the animals with whom we share our world.

Contents

CHAPTER ONE

Steady as it Goes

It's not easy being a fish with bad eyesight. I can't see the barracuda roaming our reef to make me and my kind his meal for this tide. For protection, we swim as a large group called a school. We number in the thousands. We boldly move about the reef where we eat the algae growing on the coral rocks. But my group put me, with my poor eyesight, at the tail end of our school. They hope that I'll be the one the barracuda chases, while the rest make a get- away.

My friend, Big Guy, leads our school. He thinks I should concentrate on my speed to survive at the tail end.

He said, "Bad Eyes, you have a gift. You swim faster than any other member of our school. When the barracuda comes hunting for us, save yourself and the rest of us by getting him to chase you. Lead him away for the safety of our school."

Yes, I want to help with the safety for our school. But I wish I could do more for my friends and be more sure of my survival. Being at the end of the school is a lonely and dangerous job.

I said to Big Guy, "You know the barracuda is a very fast swimmer and he always catches what he chases. I will certainly become his dinner if I run from the school. He will think I am afraid, weak, and an easy meal."

Big Guy shrugged his tail and went to the front of the group. There he led us to a break in the reef where there was a green patch of food waiting for us to enjoy. As usual, I am still the last to reach the feeding area, and as usual there is little to nothing left for me to eat. If this goes on much longer, the barracuda won't find me very tempting. I seem to be getting smaller with the passing of each tide.

But for all of my trouble as the tail runner of our school, my friend, Big Guy, came back and saw that I had little to eat.

He said, "Bad Eyes; I am sorry that not much was left for you. Maybe with your great speed, you can zip up to the sky above and find something there to eat?"

Hmmm. I stared upward to the top of our world. There were ripples, foam, and leafy palm branches floating along the sky, and it was crowded with small fish, and algae clumps! Could this be my survival?

Again I thought of more problems.

"But Big Guy, there are strange beings up there. They live above our sky where we cannot breathe. They have no fins but two legs and short arms like a crab. They are like the barracuda. Many fish disappear when they are up there."

Big Guy looked back and cautioned me.

"Yes, if you go beyond our water, you cannot breathe in the other space the strange beings call air. They cannot breathe our water and we cannot breathe where there is no water. Up there you will die and you are right. I am afraid they often deny the barracuda a meal by taking some of us for themselves to eat."

"You mean they eat us?"

Big Guy warned, "Be careful when you are near a floating island in the sky, there may be webs dangling near it. They are meant for you to swim into them, but beware, the web will catch you on your fins, tail, or gills. It is tied to their floating island. It is a terror for us. And the strange beings on the other end will pull the web up to the end of our sky with you in it. And you are meant for their meal."

I thought about his warning. Of course it would do me no good to go beyond our sky. But it couldn't hurt to wander to the top of our world and see what is there. Although I cannot see very well, I might find something to eat. And it is better than starving on the reef.

So I gave a short look back to my friend, and with an easy burst of speed from a flick of my tail, I launched myself upward toward the end of our world.

CHAPTER TWO

A Gift from Heaven

Small feathery beings with two webbed fins at their bottom paddled around the top of our sky. Then I saw their sharp beaked heads ducking down to my world grabbing at very small fish, called fry. There is no need to get too close to them.

Then, as I swam carefully along, a lot of noise came from a large dark shadow on the surface of my world. Could it be the terror from the sky? Big Guy warned our group about it. Is it the terror that drops a web of crisscrossed arms upon us and takes us away, never to be seen again?

Even so, my curiosity peaked. Our leader couldn't always be right. So I cautiously approached the terror. Then suddenly I felt a sharp and heavy wave of sound travel across my body. I darted away only to hit something square on my face.

It stunned me and I began floating up to the top of my world. The object that hit me fixed itself to my face. It had two shiny clear framed discs. They covered my eyes. Long curled barbs held them to my face and stuck themselves behind my fins. I shook my head but it would not come off.

Then I heard strange being sounds coming from the terror.

"Marsha! What has happened to you?"

"I am sorry Daddy. But when you slammed on the throttle to move the boat, I fell backwards."

Another voice sounded very much concerned.

"Are you ok?"

"I think so, but I lost my glasses overboard. I saw them fall into the water right here. I have my fins on. I am going to dive and get them."

I could tell one being was not happy about the other being doing something. It spoke with authority

"I don't think so!"

"But Dad, it is only eight feet deep here. Being near sighted, with my glass face mask, I think I can see well enough."

"Ok, you are a good swimmer with plenty of snorkeling experience. But you get only one chance. We can always buy you a new pair when we get home."

After all of that strange being noise, I was thinking the object that stuck on my face was a problem. I felt different. I realize now that this thing that fell onto my face is helping me to see better.

I am amazed. I can see far distances, well enough to spot any barracuda on the prowl. Even the terror far above is no longer just a blurry cloud. And I see the strange being faces looking down toward me from above our sky. They seem excited and are pointing their arms at me.

Then suddenly, one of the smaller beings joins me in my space. It has fins attached to its crab like legs. As it swims, its long silky threads atop its head sway in the water like seaweed. It also has large shiny eyes on its face that do not look like its skin.

It swims deeper in circles toward me. But it does not see me in the distance. It is swimming away from me and from its safety by the terror. And I can now see a giant barracuda cruising toward us.

I should help this being. If I dart up to it as fast and as hard as I can, I can lead it back to the terror. But instead it went back to the sky and the terror without me. It is a good thing the strange beings cannot breathe in our space.

Still, my curiosity captured me. If I swim to the sky and lay on my side I can better see this strange creature. As I rolled over the top of a gentle wave, another strange thing struck me. Not knowing what they were saying, I could again hear the strange beings speaking to one another.

The largest creature yelled, "Marsha! Did you find your glasses?"

The small creature moaned, "No, I lost them. Those were my only glasses for this vacation and for this trip I can't see well without them."

I understand why the small being was sad. She must need to see with those clear shiny things that fell from the terror and onto my face.

Well, I just couldn't keep what wasn't mine. So I jumped out of my space above the sky and yelled, "See me, I have your clear shiny things. Come back to my world and I will give them back to you."

"Daddy did you see that fish jump out of the water?"

"No Marsha, I was checking our boat's fuel gauge."

"That fish was wearing my glasses and making all kinds of noises to get my attention."

"Dear Marsha, you must be imagining things. Fish don't wear glasses."

To my astonishment, I could suddenly understand what the little being was saying, and I knew it was looking for me in my world.

So I swam back up to the top of my sky and swished my tail and splashed around where I almost could not breathe.

"Daddy, there is the fish again on top of the water. See, See, it is wearing my glasses."

"Marsha, you are right, it is wearing your glasses, and it seems to be waving to you."

"Wait, I will get my net and we can catch the fish to get your glasses."

"No Dad! You may hurt him."

"Marsha, it is just a fish, we eat them all of the time. And why do you think it is a him?"

"Daddy, I don't know. I just feel it, and I feel as if it wants to help me. Let me jump back in and see if the fish will give me my glasses."

"Marsha, I'm not sure about your feelings, but you are without any danger from a schooling reef fish. The Hawaiians call them Manini. So I think it is ok for you to find out for yourself. Go ahead."

More than I expected, the silky haired being jumped back into my world. There it was, in front of me. And even with its glassy eye covers I could see it wanting to meet with me. It even had a smile and I felt it was like a she of our school.

Now across from each other, as I look the being straight in her eyes, I think to begin speaking from my mind, "My name is Bad Eyes. For some strange reason what fell from the sky fixed upon my face. I believe it is a miracle to help me see better. With it I can help my school survive on the reef. But I think that you and I have the same poor eyesight. I would like to give back your shiny eye covers."

Without moving her lips I can hear her say, "My name is Marsha. I can hear your strange noises, but more than that I can understand your thoughts. Can you hear my thoughts?"

I nodded up and down in gleeful agreement and she smiled again. The strange being from another world hears and understands my words in my language and I understand hers.

As the strange being's face reddened, she hurriedly spoke again.

"I believe we have become friends. You are willing to return my glasses even though you need them as much as me. Friends should help each other. As your friend, please accept my glasses as a gift."

Then with her cheeks beginning to bulge she said, "I cannot be here with you any longer. I must go back to my world to breathe."

"Goodbye Marsha. Hopefully I will see you again. And I thank you very much for your gift."

With a burst of bubbles, my new friend Marsha shot up to the sky and out of my world. Yes, her name is Marsha, and those shiny things she gave me are called glasses.

CHAPTER THREE

Marsha Tells Her Dad

The bigger strange being was at the edge of the terror in the sky waiting to grab Marsha as she burst out of the water. I can hear them but cannot understand what they are saying to each other.

"Marsha! Are you all right? What happened down there? You were gone for two minutes and I was ready to dive in after you"

"I'm ok Daddy. I just need to catch my breath."

"What happened to your glasses?"

"Oh, I saw them, but couldn't take them away from the fish that I saw. It looked like he needed them. So I said he could keep them."

"Marsha, this is hard to believe. How can you talk to a fish under water? And since when do fish need glasses?"

"Oh Dad, I am not making this up. We didn't really talk. It seems we are talking with our feelings that somehow come as words in our minds."

"Hmmm. I think I can almost agree. After all of my years boating, fishing, and diving I can say that at times I felt the same way, especially with dolphins who would come up to my boat and chatter at me, maybe just to say hello."

"Yes Dad. It is like that for me. Do you think we can come back here next year? When we go home, can I take scuba lessons so that I can breathe underwater and better explore this mysterious reef?"

"My dear daughter, it would be my pleasure to be your scuba instructor and yes we will return to this reef next year. For the both of us, we would like to meet your fish friend again. By the way, does your fish friend have a name?"

"Yes Dad. His name is Bad Eyes"

As for me, I watch with misgiving as the wake of the terror travels against the sky in the distance. I hope she can hear me say, "Thank you again for your gift, strange being. With my new eyes I can provide a very watchful eye for the barracuda."

CHAPTER FOUR

Bad Eyes Meets Goliath

Thanks to Marsha, I have new eyes to better see around and beyond the reef. I must find my friend Big Guy and tell him and my school of my good fortune.

With joy in my heart as I swim at my greatest speed, I see my school rounding the edge of the reef. At once I scurried to the head of the group and called to my friend.

"Big Guy!"

"Whoa, little fish! Who are you?"

"It's me! Bad Eyes!"

"Bad Eyes? What is that awful thing hanging on your face? It makes your eyes so big!"

"This thing is Marsha's glasses. She gave them to me to see better."

"Who is Marsha?"

"Marsha is a strange being. She met me in our world. She gave them to me after her glasses fell into our world and onto my head. She could see that I could see so much better and she gave them to me as a gift."

"Whoa, you are talking to a strange being in our language in our world? That cannot be.

And what are glasses and what do they do?"

"It is true, we knew what we thought. And I can prove to you that my gift works. These shiny discs greatly improve my ability to see far away things. Ask me what to see in the distance and I will describe it for you."

"This is nonsense. But ok. Look over the edge of the reef and tell me what you see."

"Big Guy, I see a long dark shadow coming up from the bottom."

"Bad Eyes, your eyes are still bad. I don't see any long dark shadow..... Wait! I see it now, it is a barracuda, the biggest one I have ever seen. It must be Goliath, the leader of the barracuda school when they go on a hunt."

"From here, he looks to be fifty times our size. Quick, we must turn the school to the shallow side of the reef. Goliath is too big to follow us there."

Once on the shallow side of the reef, Big Guy paused the school and turned to me.

"Bad Eyes, we owe you our thanks. I find your glasses to be incredible. I must admit, it is a miracle for you to speak with a strange being from beyond our world. Few strange beings show any sympathy for us reef fish other than to take us for a meal. This is truly a wonderful mystery of mysteries."

"Big Guy, Marsha is gone, but she said she will return. Till then my job is to help protect the school. I will patrol each side of our school to look ahead for danger."

Big Guy with a smile said, "You are a great friend. You are still Bad Eyes but you now have a last name. It is With Glasses."

I then looked to the edge of the reef. The tide is going out and our school needs to get back to deeper water.

"I will go and scout the deeper water and return."

With Big Guy's nod of approval and with new confidence, I shot with a great tail lash into the deep side of the reef. Then suddenly a scary, menacing voice came into my mind loud and clear.

"Where are you going so fast, funny little fish?"

I looked above me to see the giant head of Goliath. His teeth, sharp as knives, hanging out over his jaws froze me with fear. Stunned and scared, I could say nothing.

"Don't worry little fish," he said with a smile. "You are much too small for me to bother eating. But all barracudas are curious, and I am wondering about those shiny discs that cover your eyes, and make them look so big. Tell me about them"

"Oh, Mr. Goliath, there is not much to say. They fell from the sky onto my head and they help me see better."

"Oh, is that so? And with them covering your eyes, how much better do you see?"

"Oh, I can see great distances With them I can help my school find their way and warn them of danger."

"Ah yes", said Goliath, showing his spiked teeth with a sly smile, "that seems to me very helpful in many ways. Perhaps you could help me find my way as well? I often get lost looking about the reef."

If it is possible, I think it is a good idea to be friends of one of the fiercest predators on the reef. But can anybody truly be a friend of this giant barracuda? He can eat me with a single bite.

"Well, Mr. Goliath, I would be happy to help you at this time, but I am scouting for my school so that they can come back from the shallows with the outgoing tide."

"Very well, for now I will go about my business off the reef to the deeper side. I will look for you at this same place tomorrow."

As quickly as Goliath appeared over my head, he suddenly and quietly disappears into the deep dark part of our world. And it is with a great deal of relief that I am able to swim back to my school.

"Big Guy!!! Guess what happened to me?"

"Oh, Bad Eyes! Where have you been for so long. The water is getting very shallow and we need to swim to the other side of the reef, now!"

"Well, I met and talked with Goliath."

"You What?"

"Yes, and he didn't try to eat me. He went back to the deep side until the next tide to let us make it back safely to the other side of the reef."

Big Guy doubted Goliath's promise to return the next tide. He pondered a thought and said, "You know, Goliath was being very nice to you. But don't you think he is really being clever, pretending to leave, so that he can come back with his school and eat all of us as we move out of the shallows?"

"Hmmm. I never thought about our meeting that way. If that is his plan we need to make our own plan to fool him."

Big Guy grimly replied, "Easier said than done."

"Big Guy, we can confuse their school by coming close together and weaving back and forth."

"Oh, what will that do?" replied Big Guy.

"Our stripes will come together. We will look like a giant fish, bigger than them."

Big Guy complained, "Yes, our school is our place of safety, but do we have to dance?"

My confidence just keeps growing as I smiled and said, "Yes, you will lead the main school moving in the center and dance from side to side and into circles. I will move a small squadron of the fastest fish to the right with another one on the left to act like a giant tail fin."

"If they approach us we will splash around like the stormy waves above. They will chase us as we dive around and up and down and waste their effort and then we will finally split up to get back into the reef crevices for safety."

Big Guy has no choice but to accept my plan. We need to leave the shallows. And he knows Goliath is waiting for us just off of the edge of the reef. So we formed up and Big Guy signaled the school to start first weaving right and then weaving left, then up and down.

A school of barracuda with Goliath in the lead suddenly appears and they launch themselves like a giant spear at Big Guy's lead school. The barracuda swim closely side by side in a tight formation.

They shoot through Big Guy's school in hopes of breaking each of us away from the school for an easy capture.

To close the gap I yell, "All fish in my tail of the school, we need to dart to the right, fast and now!"

As we closed the gap around the barracuda school, Big Guy's school dived to the safety of the reef cracks and crevices. With Goliath in the lead, his school of barracuda founders from side to side, circling and looking everywhere, bewildered and sadly disappointed with our disappearance.

Then Goliath yelled with a crushing mental wave. "Come out, I know it is you with your Marsha's Glasses."

My reply is of course respectful. "Goliath, like you said, I am not worth eating, but your friends, I think, would like me for a snack. You have certainly disappointed them."

Goliath, again yelling at his greatest mental power, "I will catch you and your school yet. We will meet again and we will be ready for your tricks."

Diving at maximum speed I met our school in a deep crevice that leads to our resting place where we will stay until the next light.

We swim with much pride at beating the barracuda school at their own game. We went on, almost as if a blanket covering the ups and downs of the coral, going happily unnoticed and safe again.

Big Guy came along side of me and said, "Bad Eyes with Glasses, you are our hero. From this tide on you will lead our school in front of me as second in command."

"Big Guy it is an honor. Thanks to the miracle of Marsha's Glasses I can now help our school better than ever. Being a fish with glasses is hardly a bad thing for me. It is a great gift to see better."

For the twelve highest tides to come, I continue to provide my excellent vision to guard the school as it ranges along the reef. With each highest tide I hoped to see Marsha again.

CHAPTER FIVE

Marsha Comes Back

As the tide comes in, my school moves to graze on the algae in the shallow waters. Scanning the reef, I see a terror approaching our area. It stops and with a heavy splash a large shiny object with two sharp hooks drops to our reef and catches on a crevice. Terrors often drop a web to trap members of our school and take them up to their world. This requires my cautious investigation.

As I looked up just beneath the terror, another heavy splash nearly hit me as it entered our world from the sky. To my great surprise it is Marsha wearing a strange cover on her face and a large black object strapped on her back. There she is with her silky hair swaying in the current of the tide.

Yelling louder than ever in my mind, "Marsha! I have missed you." Even with that strange thing in her mouth I recognize a greeting smile in her eyes.

"Bad Eyes, how are you? It is so good to see you again. I want to show you my new scuba equipment."

"What is scuba?" I asked.

"Well, I keep a supply of air from above in the tank on my back. I can stay in your world up to an hour longer by breathing from my air supply.

"Oh that is great. You can swim with me as I guide my school over the reef."

Marsha is a great swimmer with those blue things on her legs. She looks more like a fish that way too.

As we gently move along with the current of the incoming tide, suddenly, we encounter an almost invisible web. How can that be? There is no terror to be seen in the sky that put it there. Then Marsha called to me.

"Bad Eyes. Help me. I cannot move with this net that caught my tank."

"Net? That is a web from a terror. They use it to capture members of our school."

"Like your school, it has captured me. I can't get out of it. Can you use your mouth to chew the net open for me?"

"I have teeth, but there is too much for me to cut through the web by myself. We need help. I will get Big Guy and the school. Together we can free you."

"Pleas hurry Bad Eyes. My air supply will not last much longer."

I put my tail and fins to work at their best speed. My friend is in danger and I must help her. Speeding over to the last rill in the reef, my school came in sight with Big Guy in front.

I slammed into Big Guy.

"Hey, Bad Eyes with Glasses. what is your problem?"

"Big Guy, I need the help of the school to free my friend from above the sky. Marsha is caught in a web and cannot get out."

"Well, what can we do? And how can she be alive in our world?"

"She carries extra air from above in a tank on her back. They call it scuba, and it helps her breathe while in our world. But she can't last much longer. She said I could bite my way through the web to free her, but there is just too much for me alone to chew."

Big Guy replied, "Your friend, Marsha, and her glasses, have saved our lives many times."

"We will help her as best we can. We have never bitten the web to save our trapped school members, but we will try."

Big Guy signals the school, and in a flash, thousands of our members in a great swarm dart across the reef to save Marsha.

Once there, Marsha, barely awake, waves for us to help. Our school begins biting the web, again and again. In only a few moments, after thousands of bites, to our great surprise and joy, parts of the web shake loose from Marsha.

Marsha with her eyes wide open, looked at me and said, "Thank you Bad Eyes. I must go to my world before I cannot breathe."

Marsha with heavy fin thrusts, quickly forces her way up through the sky. She instantly jumps from the water onto her terror island.

As Big Guy and the school watch Marsha leave with great speed he said, "Your friend left us another present. We now know how to save our members from the web if there are enough of us to chew through it."

CHAPTER SIX

Marsha and Her Dad
Help the Reef

"Marsha! I was getting ready to put on my tank. You are barely breathing. Are you all right?"

"Yes, Dad. I got trapped in a fishing net. My tank and valve knob got hung up. When I turned over to release it, the net wrapped around me. I could not move after that."

"Well, thankfully you did get out of the net, but by what great mystery?"

"Dad, I have to thank my fish friend, Bad Eyes. He met me down there and when I got myself caught, he went to get his school to come and chew the net to free me."

"Marsha, this is a miracle, but I fear no one will believe it."

"Dad, you do believe me don't you?"

"Marsha, I am a marine biologist. I always look for facts to find an answer to a question, facts that can be proven by others. Yet

I see that your tank and gear are covered with broken net pieces and the edges are rough, as if chewed instead of cut by a knife."

"Yes Marsha, I believe you. But I need to go back with you to where this net is located. The net may be wrongfully placed or carelessly abandoned and will offer more danger to other divers, fish, and turtles."

Happy that Marsha is back to her terror in the sky, I was just leaving to return to the school. Then strange noises like a whirring and thumping made Marsha's terror island rattle. I look back and a few minutes later long blue floppy fins on the bottom of the legs of two strange beings are dangling in our water. Then the two beings then jump into our sky.

One being was Marsha. The bigger being swimming with her must be the being she calls Dad.

At the pile of the webbing Marsha points to the giant hole that my school chewed open to free her. The big being and Marsha then swim around the web and find a white skin attached to a red ball. The big being takes it and swims back to the terror island in the sky.

But Marsha lingers on the reef. I think she is looking for me. So I swim out from behind a coral tower where I was watching them. I could already hear Marsha talking to me as I came near her.

"Bad Eyes!" She said, "Both my Dad and I thank you and your school for saving my life. My Dad has found the name of the being who placed the web where I was caught. He cares about the reef as a home for many different sea animals and other swimmers like me. I think he can do something for you and the school, and other fish and turtles that share the reef as a home."

With that last statement Marsha waves good bye with her arm and points to her island in the sky saying, "Dad and I will return."

As she swims away and climbs aboard her terror in the sky to be with her Dad, I wish her the best and turned back to the edge of the reef to join my school, knowing that Marsha is on our side for the safety of our reef.

"Dad, What can we do with the owner of that dangerous net?"

"Marsha, what entangled you is called a gill net. It captures all sea animals by snagging their gills when they try to pass through it. But the gill net does not have a sign that says we only want one kind of fish. It traps all of the different kinds of fish that move in the water, even turtles with their flippers."

"They all die in the net, but fishermen throw back the dead unwanted fish. Their lives are wasted and the future of the reef and all of its members are threatened. With none of the different fish surviving, even the reef's living corals begin dying."

"Too much net fishing destroys the balance of life among the animals on the reef who in the end keep the reef healthy."

"Some fish, like your friend Bad Eyes, eat the algae on the reef and in doing that they are grooming it to keep it from overpowering the corals, which are also living animals on the reef. The living corals provide the rocky structure for the reef which also provides a home for many different reef fish."

"By the same token, other fish eat the groomers, like Bad Eyes and his school, to prevent them from becoming too many and over grazing the reef of the algae which also provide food for the reef's other fish."

"Dad, how can we help all of the reef dwellers?"

"Marsha, we will go back and talk to the officials involved with reef protection and fishing rules. We will ask them to help keep the balance of life for your friends with more and better rules for us human beings.

"But for now, let us keep your experience with the net a secret, especially about your friend Bad Eyes and his school and how they helped you. Some people might not believe you. And that kind of response hurts our chances of helping your friends."

With their hook on the reef up and the island roaring, I watch as Marsha's island moves to where the water ends. She looks back at the reef and passes a thought to me. "Dad and I will return." Then I can hear her say, "Dad, you are the greatest."

CHAPTER SEVEN

More Danger From a Web

Huddled together, side by side, the members of my school graze methodically across the reef slowly moving in the same direction. We now feel larger than ourselves and safe from predators like the barracuda. We even know enough to avoid other webs floating listlessly near the bottom, like the one that caught Marsha.

Then suddenly the biggest web that I ever saw dropped down from above to engulfs us. All sides of the web, with heavy balls attached to them came down at nearly the same time. Those of us up front escaped while the rest panicked and swam backward and sideways into the web.

Many of the school wildly struggle to free themselves but their gills and fins snag with fine lines of the web. Big Guy screams, "Bad Eyes! What can we do to save our school?

I replied, "How many of us have escaped? If there are enough of us, we can chew the net to free them, the same way we saved Marsha."

Big Guy swam outside and around the web to investigate. Coming back, he said, "There are too few of us to chew through the web."

All that we could do is watch stunned and helpless as the web hauled our captured school to the sky and the terror island. Once out of our water onto their island they will soon die from a lack of our water to breathe. Devastated, those of us left behind automatically retreat to safety in a reef crag.

Big Guy looking at all of us said, "Our hearts are heavy with the loss of our school. We will miss all of them, our friends, brothers and sisters. But we must go on living our lives."

"It is now time for us to come together, move to an outer reef edge shelter and become mothers and fathers, to spread and fertilize thousands of eggs for a new generation of Manini to form another school. With as many children as we can foster and help come of age, our school will come back to groom the reef and keep our reef community for all of us."

Big Guy looks at me. With a great thunder in his voice he said, "Bad Eyes! It will be your new job to scan the sky as well as the reef. Look for web dropping terror islands moving above us. Warn us of their presence. For in seconds, a web can be upon us. And your warning can save many of us."

After almost twelve highest tides, we had tens of thousands of children and they now swim with us, the youngest on the inside of our school for protection until they are adults. Once again we move proudly along our way as we groom the reef to keep the coral healthy and growing.

But the terrors from the sky come by, again and again. A web surely falls, but each time fewer and fewer of us are caught. My eyes with Marsha's glasses, now also looking up into the distant sky, give me the opportunity to warn the school before a web drops.

We still have a healthy fear. But no longer in confusion, we learn to survive. In formation, we zip at our best speed in the one direction where the web falls last, leaving for a few seconds a large opening to escape. Still, a few of us are always caught. Always, it seems, enough for the terror islands and web to return for more.

I never know what else might happen. Other dangers may lurk in the shadows of the reef and my job does not end with just watching for Goliath and terror islands.

CHAPTER EIGHT

Bad Eyes Encounters Black Tip

My usual patrol of the reef for the school rarely changes from tide to tide. This time I see in the distance new visitors arriving from the deep side of our reef. They are looking about and are moving into our shallows. Very sleek they move slowly and deliberately as they pass every opening in the reef. All of their fin tips are colored black. And their streamlined body has a grey top and a white bottom.

Puzzled, I hastily swim back to ask Big Guy about our new visitors.

Big Guy took one look in their direction and shudders a woeful response, "Those are sharks. They are scouting our reef. I fear that they plan to stay. They hunt in groups. They attack swiftly, sometimes spinning around and digging into crannies and holes.

I asked, "Why are they coming here?

Big Guy murmured, "I don't know. We are a small, shallow reef with not much of us for them to eat."

"Well then, maybe I should go and ask their leader what they are doing here?"

Big Guy's face grew stern with that "watch out" look of his.

"You are fast, but if they want to make a meal of you, they are faster. Beware. They have two rows of very sharp teeth running all along their very large mouth."

"I will be careful. I need to know why they are here. With just myself in front of them they may be friendly."

Swimming to the edge of the reef where it started going deep along the ledge, just in front of the lead shark I yelled in my best command voice, "My name is Bad Eyes, I represent our school of Manini.

"Why are you looking about our reef?"

"Aha!" exclaimed the lead shark, showing all of his teeth.

"Well, little one, oh, you are so little, are you asking me to eat you?"

"Not so easy. I have sharp spines in my tail, as sharp as your teeth, set to cut you if you try to bite me."

"Oh well, you are too little for me, not even a snack."

"OK, what I want to know is what are you doing on our reef? This is our home, the home of our ancestors, and we mean to keep it that way."

"And since when do you think you can barge onto this meager, spiny little reef? It is awfully small for such big sharks as you."

"Grrrrrr", snarled the shark, again showing all of his rows of teeth, "Remember this, little one. We sharks are the kings of the reef and we come and go as we please. But we are not here for you or what little else there is for food."

"Then why come here looking into our shallows and crannies?"

"Well, little one, uhhh, by the way, what species are you with those large shiny eyes?"

"My name is Bad Eyes. The beings from above call us Manini. We are peaceful and eat mostly algae that grow along the reef."

"I was born with poor eyesight. My eyes are now covered with a glassy frame that fell from the sky and became part of my head. And I saw you coming when no one else could."

The shark now spoke in a friendly tone, "Hmmm, your new skill is very interesting to me. And your daring behavior impresses me. You have shown courage to come before a school of sharks and then dare to question our presence. For this I will give you credit."

"I am called Black Tip, the Seeker. For generations our mothers have gone back to the place of their birth to have their babies. Our nursery is tides away, near the mouth of a river in shallows shaded by Mangroves. But now the shallows are covered with a black ooze and the thousands of small fish that used to live there are gone."

"There is nothing there for small fish and without small fish, our new born sharks have nothing to eat. Both the small fish and our baby sharks have lost a place to keep both of our species alive and well."

"We are desperate. Our generations are getting smaller. The beings from above hunt us for fun and food. Giant islands in the sky use webs laying them on the bottom or they drag them behind as they move on."

"They also capture us with hundreds of hooks with bits of fish, set on lines that go long distances. They eat us in every way and leave little for the birds or just cut off our fins and cast our bodies back into the sea for the bottom scavengers."

"To survive we must find a new place for our mothers to give birth to our children. It must be a safe place for our children to grow, with enough food at hand to keep them alive until they are large enough to join us as youngsters and to travel with our school from the depths to the reef edges."

"Can you help us find such a place, little one called Bad Eyes?"

I am shocked by the Seekers sad tale. It reminds me of the web that took nearly all of our school. We are not the only ones who live on or by the reef to suffer from the beings taking us without care for our survival. There must be something that I can do.

Then I burst out with a very loud reply. "I know a place for your mothers to go. It is a shallows trapped after the high water moves out with the tide. And there is no way to get in or out until the water comes back. It is very quiet and the beings can't get there where the water ends. It is surrounded by old, dry and steep coral."

"Little one with Bad Eyes, your reef is our last chance for our kind. We will repay your kindness and patrol the reef edge to warn you of the coming of islands in the sky."

I thought and then I blurted out with great enthusiasm, "You are welcome to our reef, to live as you live, and take as you take, as we all take of each other, but without greed or waste, just the need to survive as a member of our reef, sharing in our community to keep us and our reef alive and well."

The Seeker then asks me, "Yes you show great wisdom, Little One with Bad Eyes, but how will you tell this to your leader and the rest of the reef dwellers? We are predators and feared by all."

"Hmmmm, yes, I know what to say. But we will be helping each other in a partnership to keep a better watch for the beings with their hooks and webs."

We nod in agreement as I turn to find my school at the other side of the reef.

With my friend in site I swim by his side and with a friendly nudge I said, "Big Guy, Big Guy, I met Black Tip the Seeker!"

"You did not heed my warning. And you are still alive? Black Tips don't meet with us little fish. This is unbelievable."

"Oh, he said I was too little, but with much wisdom at hand about our reef troubles we made an agreement."

"Oh sure, and what scheme have you cooked up with this Seeker?"

"Well, we talked a lot, but they are asking for our help."

"Our help? What can we do for them?"

"They are looking for a new nursery to raise their young. What they used for generations, the beings from above destroyed with that sticky black stuff. If they cannot replace themselves, the beings taking so many of them for food and fun, will make them disappear from our world."

"In return for our help they will help us keep track of the terror islands and their webs as they patrol the deep edge of our reef."

Big Guy stops to think. "Hmmm. These Black Fins deserve a watchful eye for their large size, speed, and rows of teeth. Yet they could be our best neighbors. They roam farther out and can give us early warning about webs falling from moving islands. This is a good partnership for us and them."

"Big Guy! You mean you will help them?"

"Yes, it is time that we cooperate. We all have a stake in our reef. We are all part of the same team and teamwork is the way for us to survive on our reef."

"Bad Eyes, once again you have helped us. With great confidence in your skills, I appoint you our delegate for all of the Manini of our reef. Go and lead the Black Fins to the safe location near the end of water. We will honor their needs as long as they honor our needs, all knowing that in the end, we feed each other only enough to keep us all in place and surviving as a community."

"Thank you Big Guy, I am on my way."

CHAPTER NINE

Bad Eyes Greets a Sea Turtle

After settling the Black Tips on the near land place for a nursery, while patrolling near the edge of the reef by the sandy bottom, I happen upon a giant sea turtle meandering along. It is doing nothing, as if waiting for somebody. Curious, I swim up to the turtle and ask what it is doing near our reef.

The turtle replied, "I am waiting."

I said, "Waiting for what?"

"You are an algae eater, are you not?"

"Yes, my name is Bad Eyes. We Manini eat algae."

"Well, my back is covered with algae and I wonder if you would eat the algae on my back so that I can swim with less effort. They slow me down and I have come a long way."

I happily reply, "Well, we can certainly relieve you of your algae but you must move to the shallows of the reef where we feel safer. There we will make a dinner of your algae with many thanks. But why have you come so far to this place?"

"This is not where I was born. It was at a sandy beach nearby where I am bound to lay my eggs for the next generation. But the beach is almost gone now, covered with many beings from above. They are there from light to dark to light. I have come back to lay my eggs for the next generation of sea turtles. But I am lost looking for a new quiet and dark place to lay my eggs for them to safely hatch.

As a scout for the school I know the reef very well from all sides. Then with a surprise to myself I said, "I remember a place with sand where the land ends on the other side. It is not big like the water's ends by the beings, but it has a sandy edge at the water. Would you like to see it?

The turtle smiled, "Yes, show me the way."

"But as a scout I issue you a warning. Beware of the low water tide. Do not try to leave the end of water until high water has returned. In the shallows, you will snag yourself on the tower coral and if trapped, you may die from exposure to the sun and make yourself a meal for the sharks when the high water returns to the reef."

"Bad Eyes, thank you for your help. After my cleaning with your Manini, I will graze among the grasses of your sandy bottom beyond your reef. Then I will return to the end of water and in the sand lay my eggs for a new generation of turtles. They will always return to your reef, our new home."

I returned her smile as I flipped my tail to return to the school. I meet many who come to our reef for help, but I wonder what next will happen. I hope Marsha will return soon to see how with her gift, I am able to help our reef.

CHAPTER TEN

Bad Eyes Discovers Morey the Eel

It seems I never stop learning about our home. We always comb the corals for algae and then dart into crevices to rest when the light goes away or to escape barracuda or other fish eaters. But we never look very curiously among the many small reef hiding places, that is not until this tide.

Big Guy and I cruised along one long crevice when all of sudden he stopped me.

"Wait!" he said. "Go no farther. I see danger down in that hole on the side of this crevice."

I said, "What is so dangerous in that small hole? Surely we are fast enough to get away."

Big Guy groans with distaste, "Not likely. That is the home of an eel. It springs out and with its four large fangs it snatches passersby. Once in its jaws it has another set of teeth to swallow you whole."

I said, "Well, if he is a member of our reef community, I still want to meet him."

Big Guy warned me. "Bad Eyes, sometimes, I think you can be too curious. He waits, sometimes for weeks, for a meal to pass him by. And he may be very hungry. If you tempt him you will not have long to live."

Before making a move, I need to take the time to think it out. If I am not curious, would I be bold enough to meet Marsha? Without curiosity would I have enough courage to speak to Black Tip the Seeker? My conclusion? My curiosity helps others that live on our reef. With no doubt in my mind, I need to know how this eel lives as a part of our reef life.

"Big Guy, if I approach the hole and call for the eel, it may be curious like me."

"Ok, if he goes for you, I will bite your tail and pull you out of his way."

I swam closer to the hole and yelled into it with all of my mental power, "Hello in there. Is anybody home?"

From the dark in the hole a sound emerged.

"Who calls me? And what do you want?"

"My name is Bad Eyes, and I would like to meet you".

"Nobody wants to meet me, and I don't want to meet you. Go away. You are scaring away my meals."

Without giving up I said, "That is not true. What is your name? I want to meet you. I want to know how you live on our reef."

"How I live is by eating you and any fool, weak, or dead fish, snail, crab, lobster, or cucumber that drifts bye."

I said, "Well, then you are helping the reef in that way. Come out and let me see you."

"I will not. I am not beautiful like the many fish on this reef. I have big eyes and a pointy nose with sharp fangs. I have only one fin all along the top of my snake like body. I move like a snake and I strike like a snake, but I am still a fish, just like you. And I take my catch back to my hole and stay there, to avoid the sharks and barracuda who would love to eat me in turn."

"Are you afraid of me, a simple Manini fish?"

"Certainly not!"

"You don't need to be shy either. A small fish like me cannot hurt you and I will not run from you because you are not beautiful. I want to be your friend."

"I have no friends, but it would be nice to have a friend. If I come out, do you promise not to laugh at me or run from me?"

"I promise, if you promise not to eat me."

"I promise."

In a flash, Morey shot out from his hole within inches of my face. His fangs showed with a smile and a friendly look. At first he startled and shocked me. But a fish's scary looks don't always betray bad things. I smiled back and did not back off.

Morey then bellowed from his mind again, still keeping his smile, "Well, I expected you to swim off like a dart, but you didn't. Maybe we could be friends after all. I still want to know why you are here. And what do you do, being so curious about me."

I replied with a great deal of pride, "Morey, I am the scout for my school as we feed on the algae of the reef. I look for danger from barracuda and sharks and warn the school to seek shelter. And part of my job goes to the protection of your home as well."

I thought for another second and said, "You are always here and always looking. You will see things that could harm the reef, the place where we all live."

Morey with a stern look, suddenly became a partner in our reef when he said, "Yes, you can stop by on your daily patrol for your school. It will be nice to have a daily visit with a friend. And I am always looking and will alert you if I see something harmful to us all."

"Yes, Morey, I will be happy to visit you."

Morey then replied in a very business way, "Great. But now you must move along as I am hungry and need to keep waiting for my next meal."

I backed off slowly and said good bye to Morey and with the biggest smile that I ever had, I swam back to Big Guy, who left me on my own after he was sure I was not to be a meal for the eel.

At the school, Big Guy gushed out with a joyful yell, "Amazing! No fish has ever made friends with Morey. We are very lucky that he didn't eat you."

I couldn't help smile even more. "Morey was lonely and needed a friend. And we need him to watch the reef. He is there in his hole all of the time looking and waiting. And I will stop by each rising tide to ask him how he is doing and if anything strange has happened by him."

Big Guy, now with a straight smile said, "Yes, once again you have proven a guardian to our reef. But always I worry that at some tide you will meet someone not so friendly."

"But for now just keep your eyes keen to look for dangers to our school. They are waiting for us to move on."

I was so happy to get back to my scouting, but I also wondered what other wonderful or strange member of our reef I might meet next time.

CHAPTER ELEVEN

Bad Eyes Bumps
Into an Octopus

A reef tide never ends without a surprise. I just met Morey the eel, but only because Big Guy knew his ambush hiding place. There must be other fish that I have never seen before that even Big Guy might not know about. After all, our school hides and sleeps when the light goes away. But to be safe, others who don't swim as fast as we do, may come out to hunt for food when it is dark or just getting dark or even just getting light again.

Hoping to meet new fish while scouting the reef for newer algae on a coral clump, I asked Big Guy.

"What other different fish do you know that live on our reef?"

Big Guy looked back at me as we cruised a sandy bottom area without coral.

"Bad Eyes, do you see that lump of rock with green spots just ahead of us?"

"Yes, it is nothing to fear. It is just a rock on the bottom covered with some algae."

Big Guy stopped swimming just in front of it and said, "Bad Eyes, are you sure that is a lump of rock?"

I replied, "Of course, what else could it be."?

Big Guy had his straight smile on again and I was sure he was about to surprise me with something that I didn't know.

"Bad Eyes, you are getting to be a better and better scout, but at this moment you need to doubt yourself. You need to learn that what looks like a rock might not be a rock."

"Ok Big Guy, but a rock is a rock. So what is to be concerned about it? I will swim right to it and bump it along the bottom to show you there is nothing to learn from it."

Swimming with great speed, I bumped into the rock.

Instantly it exploded upward and over my head with many legs spread out and webbed together. As it hovers there, a large head with big eyes peeks over the edge of the webbing, just staring at me. It has no fins, only those eight noodle like legs curling around from its head and reaching out to try and snare me. It is not a fish, and now I know I should be worried.

I pressed hard on my mind and spoke, "Oh! Please excuse me. My name is Bad Eyes and I did not mean to bump you. I thought you were a rock?"

The rock that moves said, "How dare you bump me? You are such a little, funny looking fish with those large glassy eyes? I have never eaten one like you and I know you cannot eat me."

"Oh please, I am a Manini and just eat algae. I only want to meet and know you as a member of our reef."

"How can you speak to me? I am an Octopus, not a fish, and I live alone and I don't speak to anyone."

With respect and a great deal of awed humility I said, "Oh, I speak to you what I think. It just comes to me because I wear these glasses. They give me greater vision than any fish and they help me to speak with all the members of our reef. But I have never seen you on the reef before. Are you new here?"

"Well little fish that speaks, my name is Alucia. And I was born here. But you are the first fish to speak to me. And as I live alone, I must say it is very interesting. I get so bored being invisible to you and other fish. I need to be camouflaged until I see a crab meal coming by. And it is safer to be invisible or hiding in my castle when sharks and eels want to eat me."

My curiosity now overwhelmed my fear. "I am confused. If you are not a fish, what are you? You have no hard shape. You have no fins and yet you glide across the water faster than an eel. And you have eight powerful legs lined with round fingers that hold things tight. You also use your legs like the legs of crabs to crawl quickly along the bottom of the reef. Most of all, your head is so much larger than I have seen on fish. And you also have very big eyes

"Aha, you are indeed very observant for such a small fish. But I have no legs, just arms that serve me well many ways. And my large head makes me much smarter than I look and my beauty comes from what I can do, not how I look."

"Not long ago, I was captured by the beings from above our sky. They put me in our water surrounded by see through walls, even with a top so that I could not escape. They thought me funny to look at and smiled and pointed at me as they fed me with small shrimp. It was at first interesting, but after a while it was very boring to see the same beings in the same way, tide after tide."

"They do not know how smart an Octopus can be when bored. We are born to wait and watch and learn from what we see. We then think about what we can do to solve a problem that may be in front of us. But we don't act in haste. We wait until it is safe to try doing it. So I thought about escaping from my prison."

I then interrupted Alucia, "How can you escape from a being prison like that? There is no water to breathe once you are free."

Alucia replied with a resounding laugh. "Hah. Bad Eyes, do you see any bones supporting me or shells or scales protecting me?"

"When the beings are gone there is still enough light to see, and I can see well in the dark. I have no bones and I can squeeze through any small opening, in this case a slight crack in the top of my prison. First with one arm at a time, until all eight are outside the top of my prison, I then squashed my head until it was almost flat to finally slip through."

"Once outside my prison, I could move for a while without breathing. Down below on the bottom of the space I was in, I could see a big hole and there was wetness all around it. I had to try getting there. Using my arms I climbed arm over arm down a pole that supported my prison. Once down to the bottom I scurried to the hole and I could taste the water inside it with my arm senses.

"It was easy enough to squeeze through the bars covering the hole. I entered a tunnel full of water that had a current that carried me to our sea water. It dumped me far from our reef but I knew my way and moved in camouflage until I found my castle and am back here. With some satisfaction for my escape I admit that I am much wiser about exposing myself to the beings from above. I will never do it again."

Astounded I said, "Alucia your skills are unique. You know the reef from nook to cranny. You can change colors to the coral or rocks or sandy bottom. You swim with lightning speed and catch with your many arms your meals of crabs, shrimp, and yes small fish like me. And you are not a fish."

Yes I am unique. I am a member of the mollusk family, a cephalopod. I am the smartest of all my species and even smarter than other species. My brain runs from my head to my arms so that they can taste and smell and work independently of my other arms to achieve my needs. I can even spray a black ink in our water to confuse sharks and other animals anxious to eat me. And my camouflage is without equal in our world although many others on our reef also use camouflage to hide or pounce on a passing meal.

"Alucia, Can you help us by keeping your big eyes open for danger to our reef including the beings from above. I will stop to visit you at your castle to keep you up with the news of our reef and you can warn me of any unusual visitors that might harm our reef life."

"Oh, little fish called Bad Eyes, I would be happy to help you. I will not only be watching for myself but I will be watching for all of the members of our reef. And knowing of the many challenges of reef life, I will certainly never get bored. After all, our reef is the best place for us to live, even as many of us are taken for food by others and as you in turn help the corals by feeding on the algae."

I could only marvel at the wisdom of this wonderful Octopus with its many arms. "My new friend Alucia, I look forward to helping you in any way and for your help in keeping us aware of dangers to our reef. It is much appreciated."

"Bad Eyes, you are welcome. We will be friends but not for long. My species lives only for the time followed by the two highest tides, and one highest tide away, I must seclude myself with the eggs of my children until they are born. Then my life will end and a new generation will take my place."

"No matter how few of them survive there will always be an Alucia to help you and the reef. So for now the light is leaving us and I must go to my castle and you back to your school. Good bye my little friend who also has big eyes, and a big heart

"Good bye Alucia."

Thinking again, my curiosity overcame what all of us fear, a predator member of the reef. If I am not curious how would I know Alucia, an amazing Octopus. Now I have the stealthiest watcher to help me with her knowledge of the reef, coral by coral, and for her generations to come.

Once again, and all this time, Big Guy was nowhere to be found to witness our great conversation. I swam back to Big Guy with another of the biggest smiles that I ever had.

Big Guy then said, "I had to get back to the school once I thought you survived your encounter. The Octopus will eat anyone of us too foolish to get too close and wander away from the safety of the school. Like with the eel, no fish has ever made friends with an Octopus. Again we are so lucky he didn't eat you."

"Big Guy, the Octopus was a she and her name is Alucia."

"She is brave and uses her brain to survive when others of us just flee wildly hoping to get away from capture. Survival in numbers works for us but survival as an individual who wanders the reef for food requires knowledge of the reef, camouflage and quick thinking for escapes to hiding places."

Big Guy replied, "Yes our school moves as one to confuse those hoping to capture and eat us. The beings from above count on our schooling behavior to capture us with a web in a single swoop."

"Although we have strength in our school we must be led wisely and be prepared to move against fear in order to escape capture. As a scout you not only look for approaching danger you must learn to avoid danger and think before moving the school in a direction that proves a disaster."

"Big Guy I have learned not to assume what I see is what it is. Many reef members live by deceiving its victims, as do the beings from above. I agree. my curiosity must be combined with an alert sense of what is before me."

Big Guy half laughingly said, "You have yet to see the many more different members of our reef. Just keep your wits sharp and fins ready to swim fast and continue trying not to offend any of them. We want you to survive to help us all to survive with many more tales to tell."

CHAPTER TWELVE

Bad Eyes Befriends Grumpy Grouper

Once in a while I steal a chance to wander away from the school. Big Guy doesn't like me doing this, but there is still so much to see and new members of our reef to meet.

This time I am going out onto a sandy bottom. Usually there is little to see, at least I thought so last time when I bumped into Alucia. Then I saw this very large fish just resting on the bottom with his fins stretched out. As I swam past him I could see his face and he hardly looked happy. He glumly stared ahead as I slowly, but cautiously floated past him.

Big Guy warned me about getting too close to any strange fish but he looked so sad that I thought I would get closer and try and cheer him up.

I said as I came near him, "Hello Mr. Fish, my name is Bad Eyes, is there anything that I can do to make you smile?"

"You call me Mr. Fish? I am more than a fish, I am Mr. Grouper to you, of the great clan of spotted ones. Just go away, whatever you are. I know you are not a fish because fish don't talk. I won't come near you because if I eat you because you look like a fish, you will pull me out of our sky."

He roared even more, "Yes, I wait along the coral or behind a rock and when I see a meal your size swim by, or struggle by, as if in trouble or wounded, I open my large mouth and suck it down my gullet in one gulp."

"If it ends up tied to a being's line from above, I fight hard to reach a rock so its line is caught there until it snaps. But sadly, too many of my relatives are captured this way. Mating season is coming soon and there are no females for me to meet and help make a family for the next generation of our Grouper clan."

"I am a Manini and we have the same problem with the beings from above. We learn how to avoid their web as much as possible and help others who need our reef as a home. Maybe we can help you avoid the beings and their lures. In turn you can help us with warnings about dangers to our reef, the place where we all live."

"I don't trust your talk. You are definitely too nice to be a real reef member. Since you can talk I believe you are working for the beings from above. They like noise makers to attract our attention and then yank on their line as soon as their noise maker, some kind of near fish, is in our mouth. Lucky-me, when I sometimes just spit it out before the being's try to pull me up."

I replied, "Oh, you don't have to worry about me. I am the scout for our Manini school and I help to patrol the reef."

"Then how is it that you can talk to me?"

"It is my glasses. They came from a being called Marsha. She said I can keep them to help me see better."

"Oh, really? You mean I can eat you without strange sounds in my gut and not get taken up out of our sky? In that case, I shall make you my first meal in many tides."

"Uh oh, you do mean it!"

The Grouper that I now choose to call Grumpy, lunged at me with his mouth wide open.

I spun around and flipped my tail hard again and again to get away from him. He swam fast but not as fast as me. Still, I was not moving away fast enough, as he was definitely intent on sucking me into his belly.

"Wait!" he said. "Go no farther. I was just kidding."

I said without stopping, "What is not kidding, is your very large wide open mouth."

My tail worked harder and harder just to keep out of his reach.

Grumpy Grouper screamed with anger, "Not likely that you will get away from me. You are in my territory and are a fair catch for my meal."

I said, as I barely started to make some distance from him so close to my tail, "You are a member of our reef community, but I will not want to meet you again without some support from my friend Black Tip the Seeker."

Suddenly Grumpy Grouper stopped dead from his chase.

In a much calmer voice, although safely distant from him, I could hear him say, "Oh, there is no need for you to bring your friend. I promise that I will never eat you. Anybody who is a friend of Black Tip the Seeker is a friend of mine."

"As for our reef, you can be sure that I will defend my territory"

I replied, "Then think before you bite on those hooks and lines with lures attached to the beings above. Right now we need your help protecting our reef and we in turn can help you with your next generation."

"Then go!, "My Lost Meal". I accept your hope for our future as my reward for not eating you. I will watch my territory for strangers and let you know by way of Black Tip the Seeker."

I said good bye as we turned away from each other. Breathing more easily, swimming back to the school on the other side of the reef, Big Guy's warning words echoed in my mind. "Bad Eyes, sometimes, I think you can be too curious."

Yes, I met a Grouper. I didn't think he may be very hungry. And I didn't think of myself as the typical bite sized meal that he would like to eat. In the end, without thinking, I tempted him and I did not have long to live.

At that thought I remembered my friend Alucia the Octopus who said, "We are born to wait and watch and learn from what we see. We then think about what we can do to solve a problem that may be in front of us. But we don't act in haste. We wait again until it is safe to try doing it."

With a shrug of my fins, I shake off my fear. Were it not for my adventurous nature prodded by my curiosity, I would never have met the fish I will now call Grumpy Grouper. But from now on, caution will test my curiosity. I almost got eaten by this very hungry Grumpy Grouper

Still, my friendship with Black Tip the Seeker will help me help Grumpy Grouper to bring his clan back to life with a better chance of survival.

Back at the school lazing on the shallow side of the reef, I met Big Guy to tell him my story.

"Big Guy, you won't believe who I met on the deep sandy side of the reef."

Big Guy reproached me saying, "Oh, no. Not again, Bad Eyes. Were you out there looking for more trouble, in an area where there is no coral or rocks to seek safety? Think a minute. You are just one lonely little fish in a world of hungry members of our reef. And those glasses won't protect you out there."

"Ok, it was Grumpy Grouper and he went for my tail after he was convinced I was not a lure on a hook from a being above. I swam fast as a dart but even with his large mouth wide open he was also fast on my tail, too close, much too close."

"My fear of being eaten would not allow me to give up. And I finally got some distance when I told him I was a friend of Black Tip the Seeker."

Big Guy said, "He lives by eating us small fish and you put yourself in his territory. For him it was not just a challenge but also a chance for his meal of the tide."

I said, "Well, I was there to help him. His clan is almost completely taken by the beings using their hooks and lines with small fish lures attached."

"He said he is the last of his clan on this reef and has no mate for fathering his next generation to take his place."

Big Guy stared for a moment and said, "Hmmm. Those Grouper are sly fish. They stay close to the bottom. They do not school except when mating and can only be captured by line with a hook. I cannot believe so many of them were taken by beings from above. But Grouper are very big and must make a good meal for them. They would need a web full of us small fish to match one meal from your friend Grumpy."

I said, "We have no Grouper friends, and it would be nice to have them help us with keeping our reef safe for all of us. And he promised not to eat me."

Big Guy choked out in disbelief. "Incredible! No small fish like us ever swam away from a Grouper and lived to tell about it. I think instead of your luck, your wits saved your day, when you mentioned your friend Black Tip the Seeker. Groupers have a deep respect for sharks.

I couldn't help but smile just a little. "The Grumpy Grouper was still very sad about all of his clan being taken by the beings above. He needed a friend and we need him to help watch the reef. His hunger got the best of him as he probably escaped the beings more than once and was no longer afraid to take me not fearing I was a bait from the beings."

Big Guy, now with a straight smile said, "Yes, you are gaining a great deal of experience, the kind that our school needs for a leader. This time you met a fish not so friendly. I am happy that you have learned to use your wits as well as your speed to save yourself."

Big Guy said as we led our school to a new section of the reef. "I am happy that you are back to your scouting. Don't worry, there is more to learn on the next tide, and like your friend Alucia, I am sure you will never get bored."

CHAPTER THIRTEEN

Marsha Returns with News

While on patrol, I spotted a terror island in the sky dropping onto the reef a shiny stem with hooked ends and a chain. I warned the school to reverse its course to the edge of the reef. I then waited behind a coral tower to see what would happen. To my great joy, it is Marsha diving into our sky. I exclaimed with much excitement, "Marsha, Marsha, I am down here in the coral."

"Bad Eyes, it is good to see you again. I have good news. My Dad has convinced the State of Hawaii to protect this reef with fishing limits and the banning of gill nets."

"You mean we do not have to worry about the web?"

"Yes and No. Our beings cannot use gill nets. They can still use other nets that allow for releases. And they cannot leave their nets more than one tide change in the water. And they can only take a limited number of catches per season."

"That is good for us Manini. And we have many new friends helping us to keep our reef safe from our side as well."

Marsha interrupted me with a caution. "I am sorry to say that not all beings obey our laws. Some break the law and continue to set gill nets at night. They keep whatever they net including young fish of all species.

"Even licensed beings may use oversized nets to increase their catch and take entire schools, like that of yours, which you and I know severely damages our reef populations. And it is often hard to catch these thieves as they sell their catch on the black market elsewhere.

Now very much committed, I said, "I assure you Marsha, that we will keep our watch out for those beings of the night."

Marsha said, "I knew when I left you last time that you would succeed with helping the reef become a safer and better place to live for all of the members.

And my good news also includes something new for me. Because of my interest in helping you and the reef, I have been accepted as a trainee for a marine biology voyage. We are scheduled to make a long tour of the reefs of the Pacific Ocean."

She stopped for a moment with a sad face and said, "But I must leave on this highest tide and I am here to say good bye. My friend, we are a team. Be assured, I will be back with many new ideas about solving reef problems including eliminating excessive takings."

Marsha, like a good friend that she is then showed some serious concern for my taking risks as a guardian of the reef.

"Bad Eyes, I am still worried about you. Keep up your scouting no matter what the new being rules do to protect you. Keep safe and be cautious when you approach strangers on the reef from above or from the deep side. In many places around the world I am told beings are ruthless pirates. I will learn what I can about them and the reefs that they pillage. When I return I will share with you how we can always be prepared to insure our reef remains a safe place. Now I must go to board my special marine island. Good bye again. You are my friend always."

Marsha rose slowly in the sky looking down at me with her smile, and all that I could do was cry with my smile. But I know she will be back and I will be here to meet her again.

END OF STORY UNTIL MARSHA RETURNS WITH STORIES OF REEF PIRATES AND BAD EYES STRUGGLING WITH MORE CHALLENGES AS A REEF LEADER

About the Author

A life long boater, Larry Golicz loves to fish, snorkel, scuba, and explore reefs and study their many inhabitants. A grandfather of five, the water continues to be a place for him and his grandchildren who have inspired this story. Now retired, Larry has the luxury of writing stories, many of which he has told at campfires with his family. He loves to exemplify the wit and wisdom in behavior and survival of ourselves in the animal world. In the end the moral of his stories is to learn about our world and to keep it the best place to live.